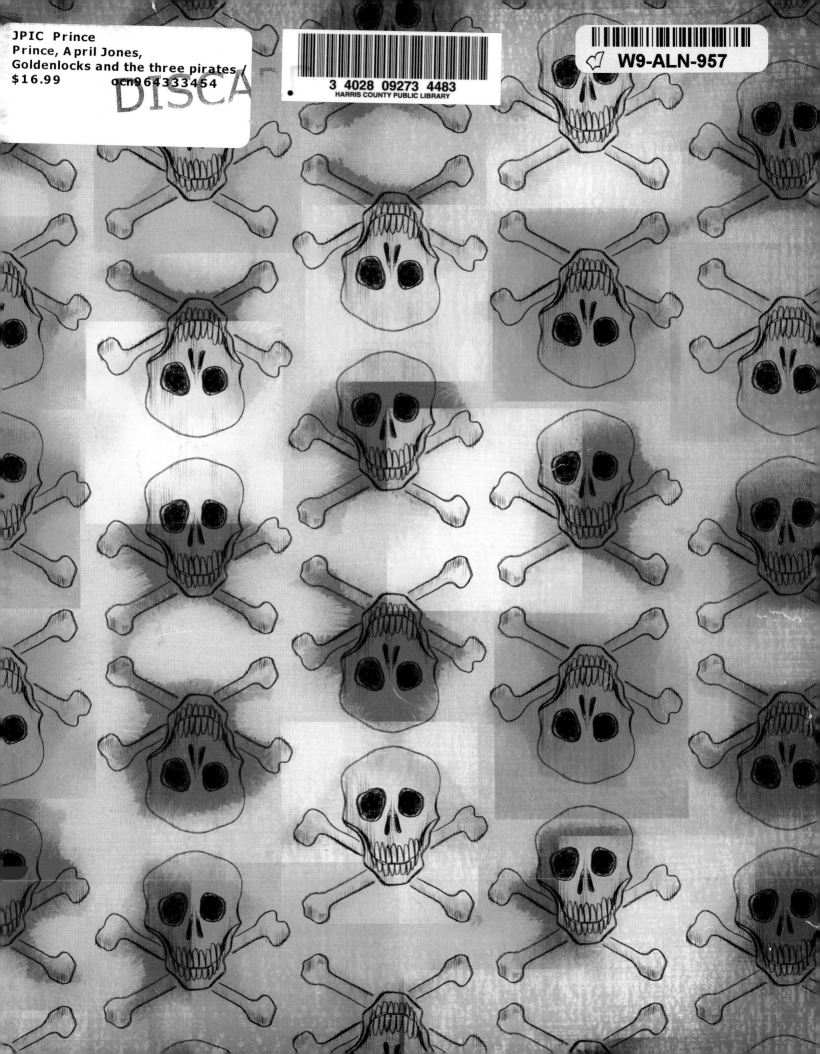

GOLDENLOCKS
and the
THREE PIRATES

April Jones Prince

Pictures by Steven Salerno

FARRA STRAUS GIROUX
New York

Once upon a seaworthy sloop, there lived three pirates.
The big one was the pilfering Papa pirate.

Arrgh!

The medium-sized one was the menacing Mama pirate.

Aye!

And the small one was the bonny Baby pirate-in-training.

Ahoy!

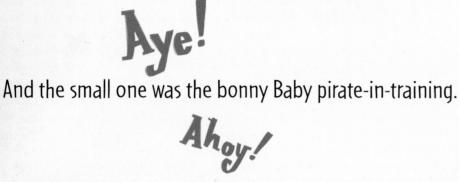

Now, Mama was cunning with a cutlass, but puzzled by pots and pans. She was clever with a cannon, but not so helpful with a hammer and nails. And her sewing—well, it was atrocious.

But one morning, Mama was so terribly tired of hardtack, she decided to make gruel for breakfast.

"Flaming blazes!" she cried as the cooking fire flared in the galley. Blobs of burnt gruel boiled over the edge of her pot. "Mama, could we hire a cook?" Baby asked.

"We don't need no stinking crew!" Mama barked, slopping the rest of the gruel into bowls with a glare as cold as an Arctic breeze.

"Aye," Papa agreed. "Heave ho! We'll row the dinghy ashore for fresh water while the gruel cools."

And off they set.

As it happened, a handy but lonesome lass named Goldenlocks was out for a row in the same craggy harbor. She caught a whiff of Mama's gruel and was drawn to the scent like a pirate to treasure. Goldenlocks followed her nose to the larger boat, hauled her anchor overboard, and clambered onto the creaky ship.

"Hello?" Goldenlocks called. "Anyone here?"

Silence.

Goldenlocks sighed. "I was hoping for some company." But her eyes brightened as she spied the three bowls of gruel. "There's the breakfast I smelled! I'm sure the good sailors who man this ship won't mind if I have a taste."

She popped a spoonful from the big bowl into her gob. "Yikes, it's hot as cannon fire!" she sputtered. "And nasty, too."

Then Goldenlocks tried the gruel in the medium-sized bowl. "Yeesh, this one's cold as cave moss and tastes no better!"

Finally, she sampled the gruel in the small bowl. "It needs . . . something." She grabbed a tin of nutmeg and added a pinch to the bowl before tasting the gruel again.

"*Yes.* To a T. Just right!"

And most of the mess was down the hatch in an instant.

Her belly now full, Goldenlocks scanned her surroundings. Never having been on a real sloop before, she was, of course, wildly curious. She ventured belowdecks, where she found three stools.

"I'm sure the fine owners of this ship won't mind if I rest for a moment," she said, settling herself on the largest stool. "Yikes, it's hard as a turtle shell!"

Then she tried the medium-sized stool. "Yeesh, it's soft as chicken feathers. That won't do."

Finally, she sat down on the small stool. "*Yes*. To a T. Just right!"

But things were shipshape for only an instant before the shaky stool smashed to smithereens.

"Ouch," said Goldenlocks, rubbing her rump. "Someone ought to fix that."

Finding a mallet, nails, wood, and some tar, Goldenlocks
set to work. Soon the stool was sturdy as a sea chest.

Next, Goldenlocks scurried starboard, where she found three hammocks.

"Surely the kind seamen who sleep here won't mind if I take a nap after all that hammering," she said, climbing into the largest one. "Yikes, this hammock is tight as a stopper knot."

Then she tried the medium-sized hammock. "Yeesh, this one's loose as hand-me-down britches."

Finally, Goldenlocks turned to the small hammock, torn and lying on the deck like a fallen vine.

"Yowza, everything needs patching up around here."

With a nearby needle and thread she sewed and stitched, and the canvas was nifty in no time. She rigged the ropes and rehung the hammock.

At last, Goldenlocks tumbled into the small bed. "*Yes*. To a T.

Just ri-i-i-ight," she breathed, and was fast asleep before you

Now, you may have nearly forgotten about those three menacing pirates. If you climbed the ratlines to the crow's nest, you'd see that they are just now rowing back home for their morning grub.

Papa, Mama, and bonny Baby hoisted themselves onto the main deck and headed straight for their breakfast.

"Shiver me timbers, someone's been eating me gruel!" Papa boomed.

"Aye, someone's been eating me gruel, too!" Mama howled.

"Someone's been eating me gruel, as well," Baby piped up.
"And most of it's in their stomach quarters!"

Mama leaned closer, sniffed, and stuck her finger into Baby's
bowl for a taste. "This has been doctored with something better
than bilge water," she mumbled. "I shoulda thought of that, that's
right good plunder . . ."

"Let's find the filthy scallywag who's breached our bow!" Papa thundered. He stomped belowdecks, followed closely by Mama and Baby.

"Shiver me timbers, someone's been sitting on me stool!" he roared.

"Aye, someone's been sitting on me stool, too!" Mama echoed.

"Someone's been sitting on me stool, as well," said Baby, "and they made it into a real *chair*!"

"That stool didn't need fixing," Mama growled. But under her breath she added, "I coulda done that . . ."

"The rogue's nearby," Papa pressed. "Me tattoo is tingling!"
Papa followed the prickly sensation, slinking toward the
sleeping quarters.

"Shiver me timbers, someone's
been sleeping in me hammock!"
Papa bellowed.

"Aye, someone's been sleeping
in me hammock, too!" Mama cried.

"Someone's been sleeping in me hammock, as well,"
Baby shrieked with delight, "and they strung it back up—
all good and cozy-like!"

Mama scowled. "I woulda got to that," she muttered.

"But why is me bed bulging like a bag of gold bullion?"
Baby asked.

At that moment, Goldenlocks' eyes snapped open to find the three scoundrels sizing her up.

"Did you mend me bed?" Baby asked.

"Did you sort his stool?" Papa demanded.

"Did you soup up me gruel?" Mama questioned.

"HOW DARE YE?"

"Why—yes—" Goldenlocks stammered. "Everything's a bit ragged around here, you know. *Someone* had to fix things."

She sat up, gathering a better view of her visitors. Goldenlocks gasped, "Are you . . . pirates? Where's your crew?"

"We don't need no stinking—" Papa began.

But a glimmer grew in Mama's eyes. "Say, lassie," she interrupted, "you're handy to a T. Our family could do with a gal like you. How's about turning pirate?"

Once upon a seaworthy sloop,
there lived **FOUR** pirates . . .

PIRATE GLOSSARY

AHOY	A greeting or exclamation
ARRGH	An exclamation or expression of displeasure
AYE	Yes
BILGE WATER	The dirty water that's trapped between the inner and outer parts of a ship's hull
BULLION	Gold or silver that has not been made into coins
GOB	Mouth
GRUEL	A thin, runny porridge made with some type of cereal boiled with water or milk; there's not much to it, including taste
HARDTACK	Hard, dry biscuits made of flour and water that last a long time but have almost no flavor
HEAVE HO	*Let's go! Put some muscle in it!*
PLUNDER	Treasure, loot, stolen goods, or the act of taking such goods
RATLINES	Small ropes strung like rungs of a ladder and used to climb a ship's rigging
SCALLYWAG	A badly behaved, mischievous person
SHIVER ME TIMBERS	An expression of surprise
STOPPER KNOT	A knot, often tied at the end of a rope, that keeps the rope from unraveling or slipping through a hole or another knot